Temple Did It, and I Can, Too!

Seven Simple Life Rules

Introduction by Dr. Temple Grandin

by Jennifer Gilpin Yacio

Illustrated by Lynda Farrington Wilson

Temple Did It, and I Can, Too!
Seven Simple Life Rules

All marketing and publishing rights guaranteed to and reserved by:

Sensory World
A proud imprint of Sensory Focus, LLC

Phone and Fax: 888•507•2193

Online: www.sensoryworld.com

Email: info@sensoryworld.com

© 2015 Jennifer Gilpin Yacio

Illustrated by Lynda Farrington Wilson

Layout by John Yacio III

All rights reserved.

Printed in the United States of America.

ISBN: 9781935567523

For Alex

Introduction by Dr. Temple Grandin

There are seven of my life rules listed in this book, but one I consider to be the most important: Work hard.

Creativity was always essential to me, but I had to work to achieve my goals. When I was a little girl, my mother and teachers always encouraged me to do my very best. There was always plenty of time for creativity, and my ability in art was supported. I spent hours outdoors, and I figured out how to fly small paper bird kites behind my bike. I tried many designs until I made one that really flew well. Endless creative play outside taught me to keep trying a new way to make it. My mother encouraged me, but she never made the pictures or kite for me. She wanted me to figure it out by myself.

Hard work was always a necessity in my house. When I was only 13 years old, Mother got me a sewing job and then when I went to boarding school, I cleaned eight horse stalls every day. This taught me discipline and responsibility as well as the pride of doing a good job. It also helped my self-esteem because I received recognition when I did a good art project and other people valued my work in the barn.

To all the children who will read this—Work hard and achieve your dreams.

May this book remind you to always do your very best and to develop your abilities.

~ Dr. Temple Grandin

Throughout this story, the narrator's words will look like this.

And Temple's words will look like this.

Temple Grandin is a very successful scientist. She designs cattle systems and is famous for her advances in animal science. People come from miles around to hear her talk. They even made a movie about her. She is successful and famous.

1

But she wasn't always this way.

When she was a little girl, she couldn't talk.

2

When she was in school,
kids made fun of her.

3

I went to hear her talk one day and got to speak with her. I asked how she came so far.

These are the seven rules for success she taught me.

5

1. Follow your passion, and learn it well. My passion was cattle, so I learned everything about them.

2. Don't spend too much time playing video games or following pointless pursuits.

Live life! Spend your time studying, and join clubs that interest you. You'll be glad you did.

3. Be yourself, but you have to fit in a little. I never cared much for looking fancy, but I learned that people in business didn't want to be around someone who was messy.

Now, I make sure to keep myself neat and clean and to always have good manners.

But, I still keep my own style.

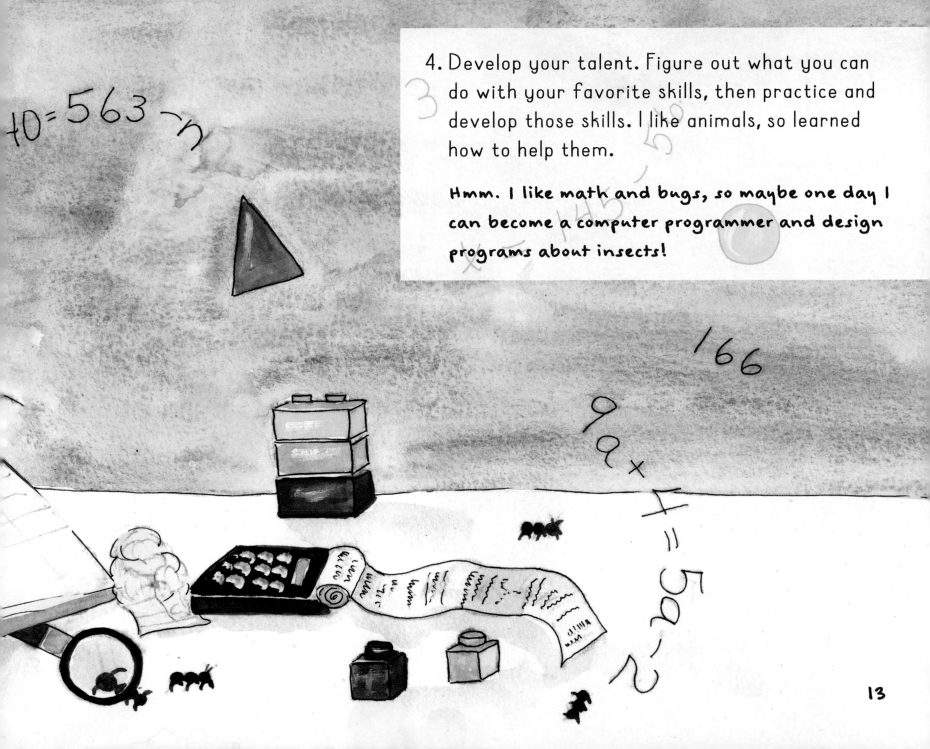

4. Develop your talent. Figure out what you can do with your favorite skills, then practice and develop those skills. I like animals, so learned how to help them.

Hmm. I like math and bugs, so maybe one day I can become a computer programmer and design programs about insects!

5. Perfection is not possible. Be good—not perfect. Learn from your mistakes, and do your best.

14

6. Work hard.

Did you know that Temple didn't start out designing for animals; she started out by cleaning horse stalls?

She spent three years doing this before she moved up to more interesting jobs, and it earned the respect of everyone around her.

7. Never stop learning. There is always something new to discover in your area of interest. Find your next goal.

FOLLOW PASSION.

LIVE LIFE!

BE YOURSELF.

DEVELOP YOUR TALENTS.

NEVER STOP LEARNING.

PERFECT IS NOT POSSIBLE.

WORK HARD.

Temple followed her rules, and now she is famous and influential in not one, but TWO FIELDS, animal behavior and autism!

18

Temple Grandin did this, and she had more to overcome than I do.

So if I try hard and spend time developing my talents into something good, someday I can, too.

19

Workbook Pages

Everyone, Every Day

Temple's rules are general life rules and apply to everyone, every day. Let's look closer at them.

1. Follow your passion, and learn everything you can about it.

Whatever it is! Maybe your passion today is insects, maybe it is trains. Whatever you are interested in, learn more!

2. Live life.

Yes, yes, yes. Go out and enjoy the world. Everyone needs alone time with books or video games, but you get so much more when you experience life, too.

3. Be yourself, but you have to fit in a little.

This is true for all of us! There are some social rules you should follow, and you should always have good manners. But, you can still be your unique self.

4. Develop your talents.

What is your favorite talent? If you do not know, you can try a few things that might interest you, and find out what you enjoy. Then you can develop that talent by practicing and honing your skills.

5. Perfect is not possible.

This is important for all of us to understand. We would love to be perfect, and should AIM for perfection on projects or goals, but be okay if everything doesn't go just right. Every mistake is a chance for you to learn what not to do next time. It's okay.

Giving 100% is something you control, and you can be pleased with yourself when you know you gave your all. Even if the results aren't perfect!

6. Work hard.

The harder you work, the closer you get to your goals. And, you feel better about yourself when you've done your best, too!

7. Never stop learning.

This is true for everyone! There is always something new to learn and experience in the world, whether it is for your life's passion, or just something that interests you.

Do you have a goal you can use Temple's guidelines on? Try it!

1. Follow your passion.

My passions include: _____

My favorite interest is: _____

2. Live life.

One group I would like to join is: _____

One activity I would like to do outside the house is: _____

3. Be yourself.

One way I am different than my friends is: _____

4. Develop your talents.

Some of my talents are: (it's okay if your talents are the same as your passions) _____

_____

My favorite talent is: _____

5. Perfect is not possible.

One time I was upset that I was not perfect was: _____

NOW, I would react differently. I would: _____

6. Work hard.

One way I can work hard at my talent or passion is to: _____

7. Never stop learning.

My next step in learning is to: _____

About the Creators

About the Inspiration

photo ©
Rosalie Winard

Dr. Temple Grandin's insights into animal behavior and her innovations in livestock handling have revolutionized food-animal welfare. Along the way, Dr. Grandin has also inspired people around the world as a champion for individuals with autism and their families. Her accomplishments as a speaker, author, and advocate earned her a place among *Time Magazine's* "100 Most Influential People" in 2010, and her life story was the subject of the acclaimed 2010 HBO biopic, *Temple Grandin*, winner of seven Emmy awards and a Golden Globe. Temple is world-famous for using insights gained from her autism to lead dramatic improvements in the livestock industry. A professor at Colorado State University for more than 20 years, she is a celebrated speaker who lectures internationally on autism and livestock handling.

About the Author

Jennifer Gilpin Yacio is the president of Sensory World and the editor-in-chief of *Sensory Focus Magazine*. Ever since her little brother was diagnosed with autism in 1982, she has been interested in how different people are affected by their senses. With an extensive career in both the publishing and autism fields, the leap to heading a company solely for understanding the senses was an easy one.

Jennifer is happy to be writing her first children's book, as this has been a long time dream.

About the Illustrator

Lynda Farrington Wilson is an artist and former marketing executive. Her talents and experiences have culminated in writing, illustrating, and advocating for children with autism and Sensory Processing Disorder. Lynda and her husband live in North Carolina with their three beautiful sons, the youngest a sensory-seeker with autism. Lynda has illustrated several books and written two children's books: *Squirmy Wormy* and *Autistic? How Silly is That!* You can learn more about her at www.lyndafarringtonwilson.com.

Here are other children's books you may enjoy!

Songames™ for Sensory Processing

25 Therapist-Created Musical Activities for Improving Fine & Gross-Motor Skills, Muscle Strength and Rhythmicity

Aubrey Lande, MS, OTR, Bob Wiz, Lois Hickman & Friends

INCLUDES CD 2 DISC SET

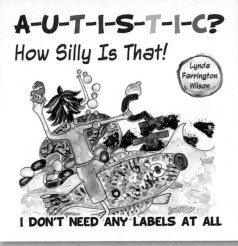

A-U-T-I-S-T-I-C?

How Silly Is That!

Lynda Farrington Wilson

I DON'T NEED ANY LABELS AT ALL

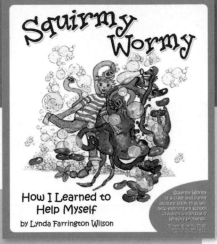

Squirmy Wormy

How I Learned to Help Myself

by Lynda Farrington Wilson

both by Lynda Farrington Wilson

Aubrey Lande, MS, OTR, Bob Wiz, et al.

both by Marla Roth-Fisch

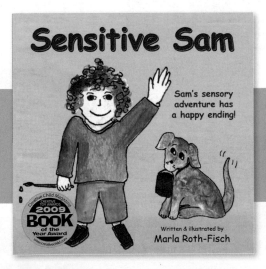

Sensitive Sam

Sam's sensory adventure has a happy ending!

2009 BOOK of the Year Award

Written & illustrated by Marla Roth-Fisch

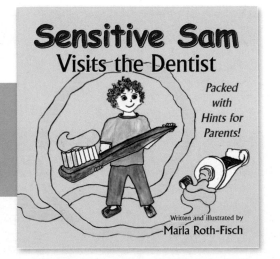

Sensitive Sam Visits the Dentist

Packed with Hints for Parents!

Written and illustrated by Marla Roth-Fisch

www.SensoryWorld.com